These Heels
Are Made For Talking

Stay positive and never give up! Bria

WRITTEN BY: BRIA P. BYRD
Illustrated by: Natasha Pelley-Smith

BEYOND
PUBLISHING

New York | Los Angeles | London | Sydney

ISBN: 978-1-952884-06-1

DEDICATION

This book is a tribute to pageantry, a sport where everyone is a winner. Participating in pageants has awarded me with:

Confidence – Win or learn... I know that I am enough just the way I am.

Friendships – I have developed many positive relationships.

Platform – I can bring awareness to issues that matter and make an impact in the community.

Scholarships – I have opportunities to win scholarships for my college education.

ACKNOWLEDGEMENT

Thank you God for blessing me with this amazing opportunity and for all the wonderful people who have assisted me on this journey. To my parents, Shelby and Susie Byrd, thank you for always believing in me. I love you both so much! To my grandmother, The Late Pauline Gaddie. Your presence is forever in my heart. To my spiritual grandmother, Rev. Herlea Reynolds your prayers availeth much, thank you! To my Godmother, Aunt Missie, I appreciate your continuous support. To my co-pastor/mentor, Nicole "Cokie" Griffin, you keep me & so many young girls inspired, thank you! My little cousins, Raylee & Ryann Thompson, your dad is amazing – Kevin Thompson, I truly appreciate you and your family! Ms. Rachel and Sophie, thanks for introducing me to the pageant world. Your kindness means so much. Thank you pageant director, Mrs. Jennifer Taylor, you said I could do it and I did! Ms. "C", I will never forget the day we met and the positive words you spoke into me, thank you! Mr. Tim and Mr. Jayme, boot camp was a great experience! Mr. Ernie, you are an awesome stylist. Thanks for all the traveling and getting me together! Mr. Michael Thomas, the best dance coach, thanks for pushing me to reach my potential! Ariel Holt, thanks for the last minute glam-up sessions. Natasha Pelley-Smith and Kimberly Haire, thank you for sharing your gifts and making this dream a reality. Cameron Wilson, Aimee Turner and Aneisha Cox, I appreciate all the invaluable nuggets you freely shared. You ladies are the true example of what the sisterhood in pageants are all about! Last, but certainly NOT least, the most awesome pageant director I know, Mrs. de de Cox. Thank you so much for the genuine love, guidance and support that you have provided me on this amazing journey. You are a gift from God!

Special acknowledgement to VIPS (Visually Impaired Preschool), a non-profit that supports visually impaired children. Thank you for allowing me to be a part of your amazing family and make a difference in the lives of others.

A portion of book sales proceeds will be donated to VIPS.

A Favorite Scripture:

"For we walk by faith, not by sight."

– 2 Corinthians 5:7

Bria is a girl like you. Sometimes she's happy, sometimes she's sad but always full of energy. Although Bria was born visually impaired in one eye due to a condition called amblyopia, she doesn't let that stop her from trying new things. She always enjoys visiting her friend, Sophie. One day she went to Sophie's house for a visit.

Sophie was outside on the big deck practicing her stage walk in heels and wearing a beautiful blue pageant gown.

"Join the fun! Put on a pageant gown and heels, Bria," insisted Sophie's mom, Ms. Rachel. With excitement, Bria put on a long white gown and sparkling heels. She went and stood beside Sophie as though they were posing for pictures. Sophie recently won a crown at the county fair.

Standing in front of the pretend judge, Ms. Rachel ask both girls what's their favorite color and why. "Yellow is my favorite color because it reminds me of sunshine and makes me feel happy," answered Sophie. "Pink is my favorite color because my mom had breast cancer and pink represents the breast cancer ribbon," replied Bria. "You're pretty good at this Bria. You should be in a pageant" stated Ms. Rachel.

Bria went to bed that night imagining and dreaming about being in a pageant.

The next morning Bria woke up and told her mom that she wanted to be in a pageant, but she was a little scared. "Trying new things can be scary. It's perfectly normal to feel that way," her mom comforted. "Just don't let the fear of trying something new keep you from following your dreams."

Bria smiled and gave her mom a big hug. Ms. Susie, excitedly entered Bria in her first pageant.

#1

DRESSING ROOMS→

PAGEANT REGISTRATION

Bria was both nervous and excited. First, was a private interview with three judges, "What is your favorite color?" asked one of the judges. Bria remembered this question with Ms. Rachel and responded, "I like pink because it's pretty and my mom was a breast cancer warrior. She's okay now. Pink represents the breast cancer ribbon." The judges continued to ask Bria questions so they could get to know her better.

After the interview was over, Bria went back into the dressing room and told her mom all about it. "It was fun, mom! The judges were really nice."

Next, is the evening gown competition. Each contestant was introduced as they entered the stage. Wearing a pink dress and a big smile, Bria confidently walked onto the stage. After all, she had been practicing this moment with her friend, Sophie.

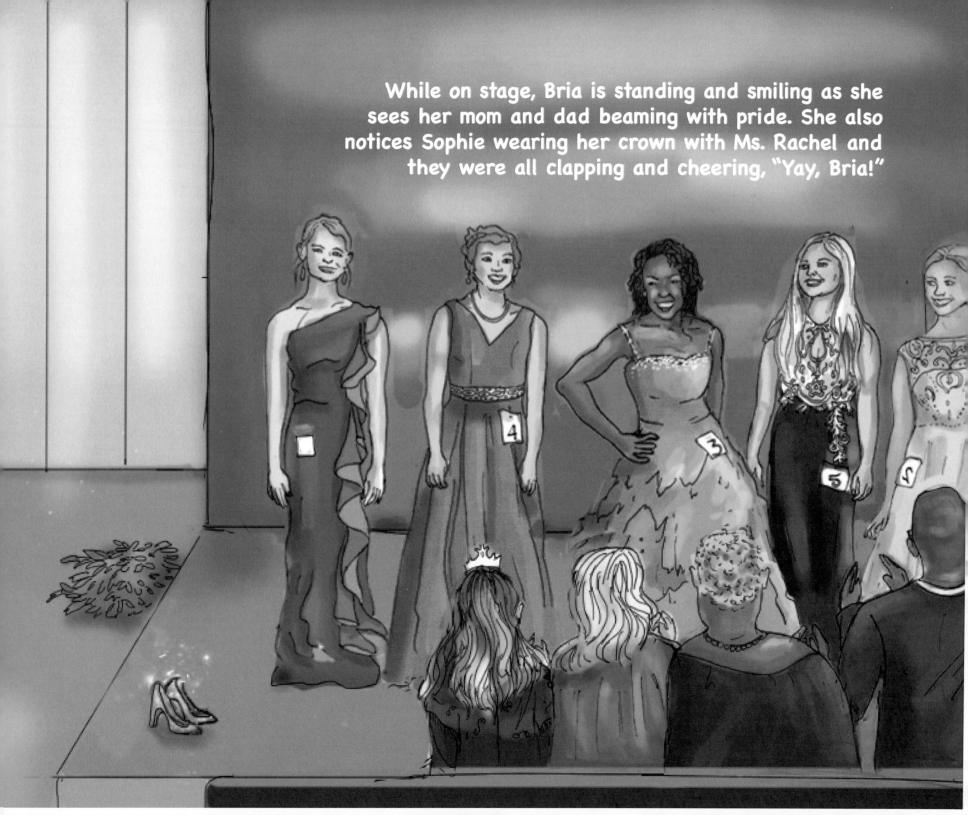

While on stage, Bria is standing and smiling as she sees her mom and dad beaming with pride. She also notices Sophie wearing her crown with Ms. Rachel and they were all clapping and cheering, "Yay, Bria!"

Although Bria didn't win the crown, she had a lot of fun making new friends. Bria's mom and dad were very proud of her trying something new. Her mom asked if she wanted to be in another pageant and with great excitement, Bria said "Yes!"

Soon, Bria participated in her second pageant. She was happy to see the new friends she had met at the first one along with friends from her school.

It was a warm, but cloudy day. Bria and Audrey, her friend from school, walked together holding hands as they headed towards the stage outside.

With all the girls lined up on stage, they each waited as the runner-ups and winner were announced. "First runner-up, Bria Byrd!" Bria was amazed as she received a trophy and flowers.

"Can you believe it? I was first runner up!" squealed Bria on the car ride home. She was so happy and her parents were very happy for her.

The pageant bug has bitten and Bria wanted to be in another pageant. "Mom, I really like being in pageants. It's a little scary at first, but it's a lot of fun and I want to do it again!"

A few weeks went by and she was entered in her third pageant. It was a chilly, rainy day but luckily the pageant was inside so the rain was no big deal.

Bria had a special guest to come cheer her on; family friend and hair stylist, Mr. Ernie. Bria was happy to see him. She sat outside the dressing room as Mr. Ernie did her hair. "All done!" he announced. "Remember to walk with your head up and don't put your hands on your hip." Good advice from Mr. Ernie.

After the private interviews were finished, each girl walked onto the stage. The winners will soon be announced. "Tonight's Miss Oldham County Teen Fair winner is contestant # 5 BRIA BYRD!" Bria was shocked, but very happy to receive her first crown and title.

Bria is greeted by her new pageant director, Ms. Sondra. She congratulates Bria and tells her she will be in touch soon to discuss community appearances and participating in the state competition. Bria can't wait!

It had been a very long day. Bria was extremely happy, but she was tired. "Your dad and I are very proud of you for trying something new and not allowing fear to stop you." says Ms. Susie Bria soon fell asleep with a big smile on her face during the long car ride home.

As promised, Ms. Sondra contacted Bria about a few community appearances that she needs to attend: A Halloween event, local homecoming football game and "Light Up Oldham County" Christmas event. Bria is honored to represent the Oldham County Teen Fair with other Oldham County winners at these events.

The next day Bria woke up feeling so grateful for such amazing experiences. Sitting in the bed with the crown on her head. Wow, she thought, I really won a crown. I wonder if this is how it feels to be a princess. In a soft voice, Bria whispered, "I'm so glad I didn't let fear stop me from trying something new." She picked up her sparkling heels laying them on her lap and said aloud,
"these heels are made for talking."

At that moment, Bria knew she wanted to share the stories of her pageant experiences and the valuable lessons she's learned with others.

A BIG THANK YOU TO THE FOLLOWING SPONSORS:

Mr. Kevin Thompson
Ms. Shewona Love
Mrs. Aliene Hardesty Kays
Aunt Denise Bentley
Mr. & Mrs. Dennis & Jarutha Barnett
Mrs. Angel Sowell
Mrs. Tera Day
Mrs. Antoyia Mallory
Mrs. Kendra Stewart Scott
Ms. Diane "Ladybug" Hudson
Mrs. Robbin Norfleet
Ms. LaTasha Norfleet
Ms. Vernice Mitchell
Aunt Fay "Tokie" Cummings
Mrs. Laura B. Winfrey PH.D. (C)
Mrs. Pamela L. Deaderick
Mrs. Monica Lacovitch, Olivia's mom
Ms. Shelletler Thompson

Ms. Denise Coleman

Mrs. Deanna Shallcross

"Little did we know where the journey and the heels would take us," Bria placed in the top 15 of 71 contestants. It has been a wonderful experience and the journey continues. "These heels are made for talking."

CPSIA information can be obtained
at www.ICGtesting.com
Printed in the USA
LVRC091301171121
703601LV00006B/13